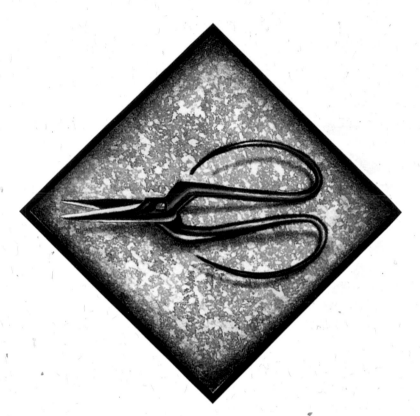

**MARGARET**
**BATESON-HILL**

*Illustrated by*
**FRANCESCA**
**PELIZZOLI**

*Chinese text by*
**MANYEE WAN**

*Paper-cuts by*
**SHA-LIU QU**

# LAO LAO
## of Dragon Mountain

*Dear Rufus,*
*Happy reading!*
*Best wishes,*
*Margaret Bateson-Hill*

**ALANNA BOOKS**

很久以前，在远古的中国住着一位老婆婆，人人都叫
她做姥姥。姥姥住在龙山脚下一个小村庄里。
龙山上，住着一条冰龙。姥姥家的旁边有一块
小小的园圃，她在那里种着菜，
过着简单愉快的生活。
姥姥从来都不感到寂寞，
因为她最喜欢坐在房子外面，让村里的孩子们
团团围着她。然后，她会从口袋里拿出一块
薄薄的纸和一把小小的剪刀，一边唱，一边剪：
"折一折、剪一剪、翻一翻；
打开它，看一看，什么最相像？"

LONG AGO in the country of China there lived an old woman.

She was known to everyone as Lao Lao and she lived in a tiny village which lay cradled in the foothills of Long Shan – the mountain where the Ice Dragon reigned.

She led a simple and happy life, growing vegetables in the small garden next to her house. She was never lonely, for her greatest pleasure was to sit outside her home surrounded by the children of the village.

There she would take a thin sheet of paper and the small pair of scissors that she kept in her front pocket, and while she cut she sang,

*Fold it and cut it and turn it around*
*Open it up and see what you've found.*

NOW, so beautiful and delicate were these paper-cuts that the fame of the old woman spread. People from the towns started to climb up the steep, narrow path to ask Lao Lao for one of her paper-cuts.

They would always find her sitting outside her house, busy with her scissors and singing,

*Fold it and cut it and turn it around*
*Open it up and see what you've found.*

And the children would watch in amazement as she unfolded the piece of paper – what would it be? A butterfly! A cockerel! A flower!

There would always be something for everyone, and Lao Lao would watch the children running home, each holding their own special gift. And as they ran, she would hear them singing,

*Fold it and cut it and turn it around*
*Open it up and see what you've found.*

姥姥的剪纸又精巧又美丽，很快，人们都知道了她非凡的手艺。
城里的人开始登上陡峭的山坡、走上狭窄的小路，向她要剪纸。
他们经常看见她坐在房子外忙碌地剪着，唱着：
"折一折、剪一剪、翻一翻；
　　打开它，看一看，什么最相像？"
孩子们一边好奇地看着她将纸打开，一边猜：这次会是什么呢？
一只公鸡？一朵花儿？一只蝴蝶？没有人会从姥姥那里空手而回的，
她喜欢看着孩子们手中里拿着他们的特别礼物，快快活活地一边唱，
一边跑回家：
"折一折、剪一剪、翻一翻；
　　打开它，看一看，什么最相像？"

NOT very far from Long Shan was the court of the Emperor of all China.

One day a young serving maid received a paper flower from one of her relatives in Lao Lao's village.

The gossip spread through the palace.

"Oh, the colour."

"Oh, it's so delicate, so beautiful – like a real flower."

"Yes," said the excited girl, flattered to be the centre of so much attention, "they say she can make anything!"

THE Emperor was a man of
great power and wealth, but
he was also cruel and greedy.
 Seated high upon his throne,
he overheard their chatter and
his eyes burned with desire.
 "Anything," he thought,
 "she can make anything…"

离开龙山不远处，是大中国皇帝
的宫殿。一天，宫中一名
年轻的侍女从她住在姥姥村里
的亲戚处，得来一朵剪纸花朵，
整个皇宫都在说着这件事。
 "啊！那颜色！"
 "啊！多精美！多漂亮！
　像真的花儿一样。"
 "是啊。"
侍女受到这么多人的关注，
有点儿受宠若惊，兴奋地说：
 "听说她什么都会剪呢！"

这个皇帝拥有很大的权势和
财富，但他却是很残暴和贪心。
他坐在高高的宝座上，听到了
宫中的说话，眼睛发出贪婪的
光芒。
 "什么都会…"
他想着：
 "她什么都会剪……"

THE Emperor went to a secret room at the top of the palace. He always went there when he needed to think.

He walked up and down the room, lost in thought. Finally, he stopped in front of the window.

In the far distance he could see the mountain in whose shadow the old woman lived. A smile of satisfaction slowly spread across his face.

He immediately summoned two of his most trusted guards. Minutes later they were seen riding from the palace in the direction of the mountain.

皇帝走到皇宫楼顶上最高处的一个密室。
他每次需要思考事情的时候，
总会到这儿来。
他在密室里踱来踱去，沉思着，
最后停在窗子前。
望向远处，他可以看到老婆婆所
居住那座山的影子。一个满足的笑容
慢慢在他的脸上浮现。
他立即传召了两名最信任的卫兵。
一会儿，卫兵便骑着马离开了皇宫，
向着龙山的方向而去。

IT was the end of a long and tiring day for Lao Lao. The air was cold. There had hardly been any visitors.

She was getting ready for bed when suddenly she heard a noise from outside that made her afraid.

"OPEN UP!" came a harsh voice. "In the name of the Emperor, open up or we'll break down your door!"

The old woman quickly opened the door as they asked, but the guards dragged her out into the night.

又是一个漫长疲倦的一天，这夜的空气特别寒冷，访客也很稀少。姥姥正准备上床休息，突然，她听见门外传来令人惧怕的声音。

"开门！"一把粗暴的声音喊道。"皇上命你立刻开门，否则便要撞门了。"姥姥连忙把门打开，但外面的卫兵却迅速把她拖到黑暗的夜色中。

UP the mountain they climbed in the dark and the cold, until the old woman thought she could not go any further.

Then she found herself being pushed up some steep stone steps.

ROUND and round, higher and higher they climbed, until they came to a door at the top of the tower.

The guards pulled away a large iron bolt and the door creaked open. Inside was a small room.

他们在黑暗与寒冷中往山上走，直至老婆婆再也走不动了。然后，她被推上一条陡峭的石级。

他们弯弯曲曲地往上爬，直至到了塔楼顶上的一扇小门前。卫兵把门上的铁闩一拉，门呀的一声打开了，里面是一间小小的屋子。

THE room had only one small window. It was bare except for a chest, a small table with a lighted candle and a sharp pair of scissors. In the far corner was the largest pile of paper Lao Lao had ever seen.

"What does all this mean?" she managed to cry out. Her voice was thin and tired.

"The Emperor has heard of your skill and commands you to make jewels for him," said the guard.

"Jewels – I don't know how to make jewels," cried the old woman, "I just take paper and cut simple shapes."

"The Emperor has ordered you to fill the chest – so I suggest you start," said the other guard, harshly.

With that they turned and shut the door, locking it as they went. Lao Lao heard them climb down to the bottom of the tower.

屋子只有一个小小的窗户，里面除了一个箱子、一张摆着一支点燃着的蜡烛和一把锋利剪刀的小桌子外，并没有其他东西。屋子远处一角堆了一大堆姥姥一生从未见过那么多的纸。

"这是什么意思？"

姥姥喊道，声音细弱无力。

"皇上听说了你的本领，现在要你给他制作一箱子满满的珠宝。"

卫兵说。

"珠宝？我不会制作珠宝。"

姥姥叫道。

"我只会剪一些简单的纸玩意儿！"

"皇上命令你把这个宝箱子装得满满的，你还是快点动工吧！"

另一个卫兵粗暴地说。

接着，卫兵把门关上，上了锁后离去。姥姥听着他们的脚步声走向塔楼下。

姥姥看了看屋子的四周，叹了一口气。很冷啊！这里并没有暖气，唯一的光源来自桌子上的蜡烛，她怎么办啊！

看来，答案只有一个。她走到那堆纸前，惊讶地看着，她从来没有见过那么精美的纸张！又薄又滑，每一张都是光耀夺目的纯白色。

"是要钻石吧……"

姥她拿起尖锐的小剪刀开始动手，可能是习惯，又可能是为自己打气，她开始唱着：

"折一折、剪一剪、翻一翻……"

但是，她的声音颤抖着，两行泪珠沿着脸儿慢慢往下流。她感到很孤独，因为身旁并没有孩子们陪着她。

"当作孩子们都在我身旁吧。" 她轻轻地对自己说。

LAO LAO looked around the room and sighed. It was cold. There was no fire and the only light came from the candle on the table. What was she to do?

There seemed to be only one answer. She went over to the paper and looked in amazement. She had never seen such fine paper before – so smooth and thin, each piece a pure but dazzling white.

"Diamonds, I suppose," said the old woman. She set to work, taking the small sharp scissors laid out for her, and, perhaps from habit, or perhaps to give her courage, she started to sing,

*Fold it and cut it and turn it around...*

But her voice faltered and two tears fell slowly down her face. She felt so alone, with no children there to watch her cut the paper.

"Perhaps if I pretend they are here…" she whispered.

折

一折、剪一剪

LAO LAO worked hard. Piece after piece she folded and cut, and the treasure chest started to fill up with the pieces of carefully cut paper.

As it came to the deepest and darkest part of the night, Lao Lao grew colder and colder. Her movements grew slower and eventually stopped. The clear black sky sparkled with diamonds of its own and a slip of cold moon shone in through the tower window, gently lighting the old woman's face as she lay exhausted on the stone floor with the cold freezing her bones.

姥姥不停地一块一块
折着、剪着，珠宝箱开始
放进一片片精巧的剪纸。
夜渐渐深了，姥姥觉得
越来越寒冷，她的动作也
变得越来越缓慢。
最后，她不能继续下去了。
姥姥虚弱地躺在石板地上，
身体感到阵阵冰冷，窗外
黑漆的天空挂着大自然
的宝石，一闪一闪地，
一丝冷冷的月色从塔楼
的窗户射进来，轻轻照在
她的脸庞上。

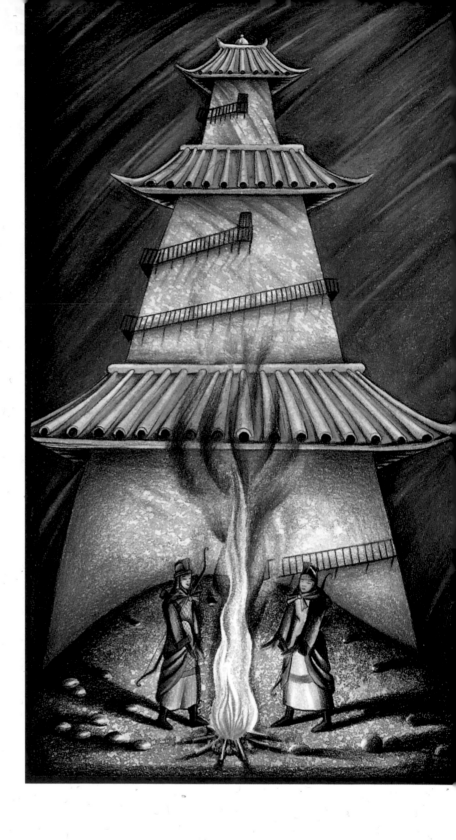

塔楼下，两个卫兵在身旁
生了一堆火取暖，
他们正在等待着。

DOWN below, at the bottom of
the tower, stood the two guards,
waiting, and warming themselves
by a fire.

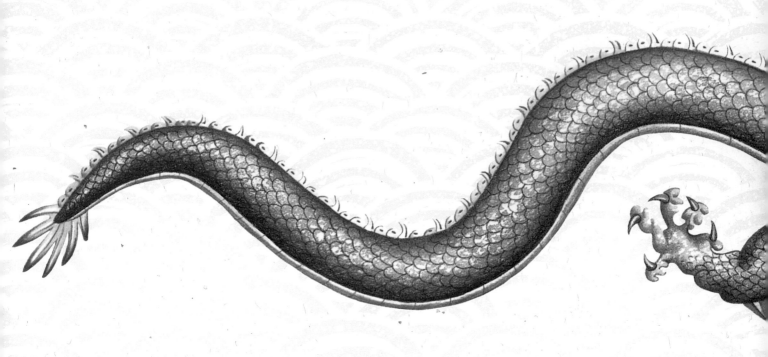

AND yet in all the darkness and stillness something was watching,
something had seen everything – always saw everything –
the Ice Dragon who slept at the top of the mountain.

Tonight the dragon knew that something was wrong…
He stretched forth his giant scaled body and, leaving his bed of snow,
he flew over the land.

Below him lay tiny villages tucked up for the night and sprawling
towns filled with busy people who had little time for rest.

He flew over the great palace of the Emperor, then, circling back
towards the mountain, he saw the Emperor riding towards the tower.

这时候，黑暗与寂静之中，有一样东西正在观看着，把什么都看在眼里。
他什么都看得见。他 – 正是那头睡在山顶上的冰龙。
今天晚上，冰龙知道有事发生了。他伸展着庞大的身躯，
离开他的雪床，向着大地飞去。冰龙的脚下，
小小的村落笼罩在浓浓的睡意中；延伸的市镇内，
　人们正在忙忙碌碌地为生活奔波。

　　　　　　　　冰龙飞越了皇帝的宫殿，
　　　　　　　然后绕回山上。
　　　　　　　他看见皇帝正骑着马向塔楼走去。

ROUND and round the tower the Ice Dragon circled,
the anger rising in his chest as he saw the old woman lying
helpless on the floor.

From deep within him came a cry – ice-cold breath streamed
from his nostrils and froze the blood of the guards at the bottom
of the tower. The Emperor fell from his horse, dazed by the sound,
unable to move.

Then the Ice Dragon gently picked up the old woman, lifting
her up high into the sky, safe from the guards, the Emperor and
all further pain.

Lao Lao's papers billowed round in the ice-cold air, and,
as they fell, they turned into snowflakes, shining and sparkling in
the moonlight...

And when people woke in the morning the ground was
covered in papery, white snow.

冰龙绕着塔楼转呀转，看见孤弱无助的
老婆婆躺在地上，心里非常愤怒。
冰龙从心底发出一声怒吼，鼻子喷出冰冷的气息，
凝固了塔楼下卫兵的血液。皇帝被这巨大的
声音吓得从马背上摔下来，不能动弹。
冰龙轻轻地把老婆婆从地上提起，
带到高空中，远离了皇帝与卫兵、
远离所有的痛苦。
姥姥的剪纸四周飘洒，纸片落下来的时候，
都变成了一片片晶莹的，耀目的雪花，
在月色中闪耀。
人们在第二天的清早起来时，地上已盖了一层
厚厚的、纸一般似的皑皑白雪。

从此以后，姥姥骑着冰龙在天空中
飞翔。她坐在龙背上，拿着剪刀和纸，唱着：
"折一折、剪一剪，翻一翻；打开它，看一看，什么最相像？"
春天，她把粉红色的花儿挂上树枝头；
夏天，她为田园铺满了鲜花；秋天，她带来苹果和果仁；
但最特别的，还是她送给冬天的礼物：
那些从她手上撒下来的雪花。

LAO LAO now rides on the back of the dragon. She flies all over
the land and whilst she sits, she takes a piece of paper and sings,

> *Fold it and cut it and turn it around*
> *Open it up and see what you've found.*

In spring she covers the trees with the palest of pink blossoms,
during the summer months the fields are filled with flowers, and
apples and nuts are her autumn harvest. But, most special of all,
as a winter gift, white snowflakes fall from her hand.

THE tower on the mountain of the Ice Dragon is no longer standing. Instead you will find three pillars of ice. It is said that if you look very carefully, you can make out the figures of the Emperor and his two guards. When they learn compassion, they will return to human form — but that is another story...

冰龙故事里那座山的塔楼已经不在了，
在山上现时可以见到三条冰柱子。
听说，如果你仔细的看清楚，
你可以 看到皇帝和他的两个
卫兵呢！不过，如果
他们能知道悔过的话，
他们还是可以复回人形的。
但那会是另一 个故事了......

**THE END**

CHINESE WRITING developed about 4,000 years ago. In the
beginning, pictures stood for objects, words and ideas.
Over a few hundred years, the picture signs were gradually simplified
into the modern characters that are still used today. There are over
50,000 characters, but children can get by using a few thousand.

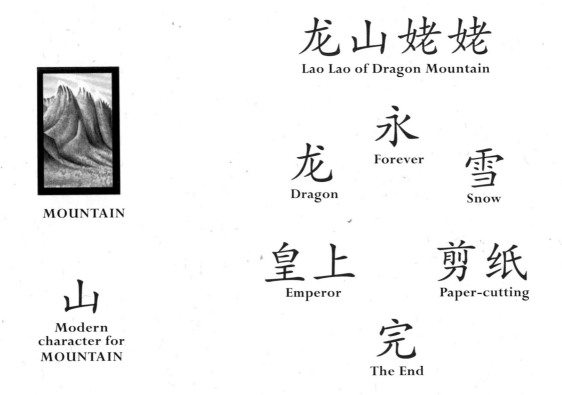

**MOUNTAIN**

山

Modern
character for
**MOUNTAIN**

龙山姥姥
**Lao Lao of Dragon Mountain**

龙
**Dragon**

永
**Forever**

雪
**Snow**

皇上
**Emperor**

剪纸
**Paper-cutting**

完
**The End**

China is a huge country and its inhabitants speak over 800 languages
and dialects. However, because Chinese characters stand for ideas rather
than sounds, Chinese people can share the same writing system.
When the book was first published, we were advised to use the more
ornate classic Traditional Chinese script – you can still see it used in the
books as part of the illustration. This new edition reflects how times have
changed. Since Simplified Chinese is now taught in many UK schools we
have commissioned a new translation from Manyee Wan, so the text you
see in the story is called Simplified Chinese.

IN CHINA, where paper was invented, people have been making paper-cuts since AD 618. The art may have begun as a courtly pastime in the palaces of the great rulers, but today paper-cutting is popular all over China.

At festival times, in China, and in places all over the world where Chinese people live, paper-cuts are given as greetings or gifts and put on display.

The BUTTERFLY, FLOWER and SNOWFLAKE designs are symmetrical so, just like Lao Lao, you fold and cut them. You will need to use very thin paper.

## The BUTTERFLY
is the simplest paper-cut to make.
1 Take a piece of paper and fold it in half.
2 Copy or trace BUTTERFLY **A**.
3 Cut out the inside bits first, next cut around the edge, then open it up.

Fold Side

**A**

You can make a really pretty butterfly by using brightly patterned paper – wrapping paper works perfectly. Trace BUTTERFLY **A** onto tracing paper. Fold the patterned paper then staple the tracing paper to it. Cut through both the tracing paper and the patterned paper – inside bits first.

# The FLOWER and SNOWFLAKE
### are a little bit more complex.

**1** Take a piece of paper 22cm x 22cm and cut it into a circle (**A**).

**2** Fold it in half (**B**), then fold that into thirds (**C**) putting 1 in front
and 3 behind so your piece of paper
looks like the diagram (**D**).

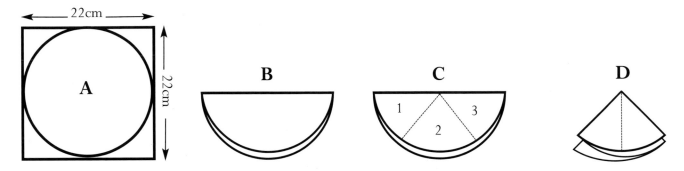

**3** Then fold it in half one more time and trace the shape **E** or **F**.
Like the BUTTERFLY, staple the tracing to your paper.
Cut out the inside bits first, then go around the outer edge.
You could use a really nice glittery paper for the SNOWFLAKE

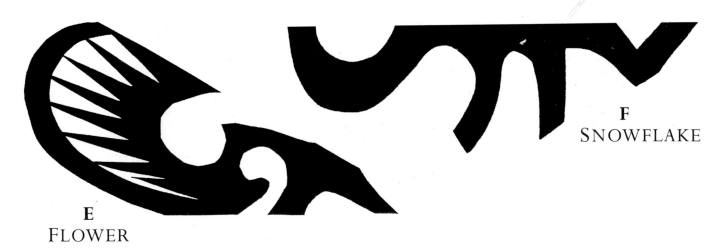

**F**
SNOWFLAKE

**E**
FLOWER

## The DRAGON (over the page)

is not symmetrical so you don't fold it. Instead, you simply trace
the image from this book, staple the tracing paper onto coloured paper
and cut through both. Carefully cut the inside bits first (the staples will
hold the papers together), then go around the edges.